ISBN: 9798637204779

Originally published: May 2020

Second Edition

Cover design by: RandomLime

Special Thanks to:
GiGi
Catherine Baignoire
Tery Lemanis
and Mark (why on earth did I miss that in the 1st edition?)

CONTENTS

For my family

WHAT'S ON

TRUE CRIME

TONIGHT?

a mystery story

CATHERINE H. AMBROSE

EPIGRAPH

Time the all-seeing has found you out,
against your will.

Sophocles, *Oedipus Tyrannus*

PROLOGUE

April 29th, 2020

My name is Ariadne Foster. What you're about to read is all true and occurred during the first three weeks of the pandemic. Names, critical personal details, and locations have been changed to protect the privacy of the survivors and protagonists. The facts and circumstances, however, remain thoroughly accurate.

CHAPTER 1

Mystery on a Train

> *"How would your book start?"*
> *"Either someone wakes up or dies."*

As I open my eyes, I reminisce about a dialogue taking place in a TGV train from Paris to Brussels a few years ago, when my friends and I embarked on a six-day long great adventure in central Europe. This brings me to today's grand adventure, the sixth day of my quarantine and home isolation. I look at my smartwatch, it's 8.27 am. My hand then reaches for the phone under the bed, the battery is running low, no notifications there. Shy shafts of sunlight break through the shutters; light together with morning silence creates a form of secure warmth. A warmth unquestionably fortified by a fluffy down duvet and a relaxed leg touching mine underneath the covers. I get up quietly, trying not to disturb Mark's REM sleep.

I switch the espresso machine on and throw a pod inside. Hot or cold? That's a new dilemma! I feel rested yet thirsty, so I opt for the iced coffee.

Ice cubes… How many? The coffee-ice crucial ratio is undervalued by many, but not me. The first sip cools pleasantly both my palate and brain. *Brain.* Funny how it works after seven hours of uninterrupted sleep and takes us back to safe places. It's been a long time since l last looked back on that trip, let alone those train moments. The seven of us on a train, playing cards and solving mysteries, what a day that was!

I recall the wagon we shared with a group of young Italian male friends who exhibited a rather peculiar behavior throughout the journey. Leaving the railcar and then coming back, sharing long, intense gazes and awkward smirks. Unfortunately, we couldn't understand a word from the little they were saying; the only clues for us were a couple of carton boxes filled with greasy fast food meals they carried and their undue mobility. The leading theory was they were involved in a murder and were trying to create alibis.

"God, I slept for thirteen hours," I hear a bleary voice approaching the kitchen. Mark is up.

❈ ❈ ❈

I sit in front of my laptop, scrolling down news and coronavirus global live updates. A few days ago, the WHO declared a pandemic, the epicenter of which has now moved to Europe, while in China, the disease outbreak seems to be decelerating. Schools, universities, and most stores have closed down almost all over the world, apart from pharmacies and supermarkets. Our government rushed into taking preventive measures last week, so hopefully, we'll keep the number of cases and death toll on the low side. New terminology is emerging as well. "Social distancing" is trending everywhere, from hashtags on Twitter and Instagram to government press releases. I have no idea which word was voted "word of the year" in 2019, but for 2020 the winner is clear, even though it's a phrase.

It seems at least six months have passed since December, but it's only mid-March. As I look back, I have no recollection of a notable moment from the past two months. Friday nights, weekends, bank holidays all erased from my memory. I get out on the balcony, and the sun blinds me as I take a look around, most neighbors are out as well enjoying the fantastic weather themselves. Maybe I'll come back later with one of the novels waiting for me patiently in the bookcase for months. Why not create a lovely outdoor reading spot? I take the last sip of my iced espresso and realize I haven't washed my face yet.

Skincare is certainly simplified nowadays. No make-up, no sunscreen needed in the house. Only water and adequate epidermal hydration form my current beauty regimen. I splash my face with an abundance of cold water and look in the mirror. My skin looks plump and fresh, I even notice fragments of healthy rose undertones on my cheeks. The hair, on the other hand, is displaying its full frizzy potential, definitely not cooperating. Overall, I agree my mirror image today is decent.

Six days ago, I experienced fatigue, and my

temperature rose to 37.3 °C. Following the government's directions, I stayed home, and today I feel remarkably better. Young people displaying mild symptoms are not encouraged to visit hospitals to get tested for COVID-19. So, home it is. Mark hasn't developed any symptoms yet. Chances are though it's not coronavirus as I've been showing such signs periodically since January, especially under stressful circumstances.

✻ ✻ ✻

The time is now 10.28 am, and I'm in the kitchen once again preparing myself a second espresso drink, this time I'm adding a bit of coconut milk. It's Wednesday, and I still haven't received any emails from the university. The pandemic caught the forensic department in the middle of two research projects, primarily funded by national grants and a few tense weeks before the Easter holidays. *Easter...* It was Easter break back then, wasn't it? Subconscious flawlessly retracts memories with immense accuracy. Generally, at this point, we'd be making arrangements for the forthcoming vacation. Only no plans, for now, just memories.

I return to the living room to find Mark at his desk as he ends a video call with his team. They've been developing a new cryptocurrency for the past four months and are currently feverishly designing a phone application.

"I dreamt so much last night. Or in the morning, I think. How are you feeling? Did you sweat again?" he asks.

"No, Mark, I'm better. Woke up revived, not used to that."

"Did you see the numbers in Italy?"

"I know. Mortality is six percent. It seems to be worse than in China." I checked it only twenty minutes earlier.

I'm lying on the green sofa now checking Twitter updates on my phone moving my legs in a random cycling mode up in the air. The Twitter community is genuinely committed to discover and expose every aspect of conspiracy circulating online. Suddenly, I get a massive wave of notifications as apparently everyone's going live on social media to demonstrate their quarantine morning workout routines. After they had an adequate quantity of wholesome porridge for breakfast.

"We are running out of cheese, bread, and dish soap. We'd better make a list and place an order, Ariadne. The online waiting list is up to five days."

"Most importantly we're running out of coconut milk," I add as I text Alex:

"Remember the Italian train mystery?"

CHAPTER 2

Friday Night

Mark is in the kitchen preparing fish croquettes for tonight's dinner. He's coughing. *Hmm...*I just ended a video call with my sister; we shared our views on the global stock market recession and commented on several videos on TikTok. How millennial of us. She sounded worried about the possibility of being furloughed in the next weeks. *As we should all be.* I get up, and as I exit the bedroom, I glance at the full-length mirror. I've been wearing the same yoga pants since Tuesday or Wednesday, which is ironic since the only form of exercise my body has experienced for the past 10 days is browsing around our one-bedroom apartment. I enter the kitchen to find the chef listening to an undefined documentary podcast.

"Is Mackenzie airing tonight, Aria?"

"I suppose so. Let me check Twitter."

Mackenzie Ferguson, a former police detective inspector who effectively shifted to prime-time television, hosts one of the most successful true-crime investigative live shows. The episodes consist of a retrospective analysis of old unsolved crimes, and experts share their thoughts on the cases. Usually, the thrill is moderate; nevertheless, it's become kind of a Friday cult. Social distancing hasn't affected its schedule, it's airing as usual tonight, in less than fifty minutes. The hashtag #crimetonight is trending already as fellow home-based detectives are gathering online.

* * *

We are dining at the coffee table as the TV is playing in front of us. Ferguson is introducing her team for tonight, a lawyer, a former police chief inspector, a forensic sociologist, and a private detective. Tonight, the show's first part is focusing on an unresolved double homicide from eighteen years ago.

Stephanie Oldman, a suburban housewife, and her mother Eleanor were found slaughtered in their suburban home by a concerned neighbor after he saw dark smoke coming out of the open rear kitchen window. He smashed the kitchen door only to discover a burnt stew and the two women lying on the floor in a pool of blood. Suspicion fell immediately on Stephanie's husband Jason, a biology college professor. Charges were never pressed against him since the evidence was inadequate; no one has been officially accused of the crime to this day. Police at the time theorized it was possibly a mentally disturbed stranger who committed the brutal murders. *An intruder.* None of the family members accepted the invitation to be on the show tonight, just a few neighbors and two of the wife's friends are joining the investigative team to answer questions and share their perspectives on the hideous crime.

Unfortunately, the evidence they can share with the audience tonight is little since the case isn't officially closed. The core of revealing proof consists of some threatening letters sent to the family, the murder weapon found on the kitchen floor, a missing watch, and a sedated dog. The chief witness, the neighbor, is describing the horrific moment he smashed the door and saw all the blood surrounding the lifeless bodies of the two women.

"He did it. The husband did it," Mark states as he stretches on the sofa. "Nine out of ten times, the murderer is the spouse."

"The numbers aren't so dramatic... Chances are indeed the women knew their killer- *or killers.*"

"Who else? Someone from the family? An enemy? What about inheritance issues? What time were the murders committed? Who saw the women last alive? Was anyone else at home?"

"Fair questions. Can you think of a couple more? Let's write them down."

"You see Ariadne, we have to answer the following categories: who, when, and why."

"First of all, *who.* Stephanie had no siblings. Her direct family consisted of her mother, husband, and three children, according to Mackenzie and the internet. The last person to see them alive was Jason before he left for work that morning. The twin sons didn't live in the house back then, they rented a flat in the city, and the daughter was at a summer camp," I add while consulting my phone.

"So, Steve Hunn, the neighbor, is the next

person who encounters the victims and enters the crime scene."

"Right, along with his wife."

"As the bald inspector said, the massacre took place between six and nine in the morning. But the bodies were discovered around noon, 12.30?"

"Exactly. Although the time of the crime had remained a matter of dispute between pathologists for a long time."

"Jason claimed he had left the house around seven that morning, and a witness is placing him at a local bakery at approximately 7-7.10 am. Who is that witness?"

"I found an old newspaper entry. Listen to this, Mark, the witness, the baker himself, remembers Jason distinctly ordering twelve bagels and a cappuccino that morning."

Mark starts laughing, "The man liked his bagels, what can I say."

"His alibi is reinforced by the newsstand man. He too recalls interacting with the husband that morning; Jason had asked him whether he could get him a certain copy from previous week's newspaper."

"Hmm... That's plenty of alibis."

"Sure. One thing is alibi; another is *too much alibi.*"

A Burnt Stew

The show is over. All in all, today's episode summed up any known public knowledge about the case, enriched with a couple of dramatically toned interviews and a few prestigious statements from the expert panel. Nonetheless, we are deeply absorbed in our investigation, which has now moved online. Our primary reference is a blog from the early '00s that had gathered most of the information, clues, even crime scene photos, and excerpts from the pathology reports.

"It doesn't make sense," he moans. "Why would anyone kill these poor women? A burglary went bad? Only one thing went missing, Stephanie's watch. What's the significance of that?"

"The husband insisted the watch, a vintage Omega design and family heirloom, was of great value. According to the blog, its estimated worth was $72000 in 2002. See?" I point at a low-resolution image of the design on the screen.

"I wouldn't price it over $200."

"Collectors think otherwise, Mark. However, its disappearance could have been staged. Why leave her earrings back? Those were diamond studs."

"What if there was something *in* the watch?"

"Like an espionage game?"

"Can't rule it out, can you?"

"What's even more disturbing is the total lack of physical evidence in the crime scene. No fingerprints, no traces of DNA. And the dog!"

"Wasn't the dog found sedated?"

"Was it? Hints of acepromazine were found in its system, but the amount of it was insufficient to completely knock the dog out. A German shepherd would have, to a certain degree, responded towards an external threat, even under such circumstances."

"A bogus sedation, part of an act, an inside job. Orchestrated by the husband. Who else would benefit from her death? Financially, at least."

"I suppose so. The beneficiaries must have been Stephanie's children and Jason. But babe, don't forget; there are two victims. Stephanie and Eleanor."

"Mother and daughter, over twenty stabs. The slayer felt such hatred against them," Mark adds as he walks to the kitchen. He comes back with two cans of carbonated water. "Remind me, what about those anonymous threatening letters? Did the police speculate who was behind them?"

"Letters had allegedly been left in the family's mailbox eight months before the murders."

"Let me guess. The husband was the sole eyewitness of this evidence, right?"

"He claimed he thought it was a prank at the time, tossed the letters away, and didn't connect them to the crime, only a month afterward."

"Imaginary letters plus fake sedation, who cross-examined the man anyway? Did police interview him at all?"

"Since neither his fingerprints nor his blood was found on the knife, I presume the detectives couldn't use a pressure point."

"So, they concluded the killer was a stranger, most likely a mentally unstable individual who attacked the unfortunate women. Let's recap, let's make a timeline," Mark stands up and stretches his hands up. I reach my notepad and begin writing while consulting my screen.

"Alright. From all the information we have, the

following happened on the morning of June 21st, 2002," I say as I show him the bullet list.

TIMELINE

- *6-6.15: the family wakes up*
- *6.30-7.00: Stephanie and Eleanor prepare lunch, as they would typically do, before engaging in general housekeeping*
- *6.50: Jason claims he left home*
- *7-7.10: Jason has an alibi*
- *7.45: Jason arrives at work*
- *12.30: neighbor finds the bodies, a burnt stew, and a calm dog*
- *13.00: police arrive and call Jason*
- *14.00: Jason comes to the crime scene, he examines the house, nothing is missing, apart from his wife's watch*
- *Homicides took place between 6-9 am (most likely).*

"What strikes me, besides the hideous crime itself, is who cooks stew at 6.30 in the morning! These ladies had a strict domestic schedule," Mark points out.

"I can't relate," I smirk.

"I know. Maybe this is to your advantage and lowers your chances of getting murdered at 6 am."

❊ ❊ ❊

I can't sleep. It's 3.05 am, I'm scrolling purposelessly on my phone as Mark is slightly snoring next to me. I think of the tragic siblings; George, Matt, and Abigail. George and Matt had just graduated from college and landed their first jobs in the city, Abigail was barely fifteen years old. I decide to look them up on social media.

George Oldman, an electrical engineer, lives in Zarqa together with his wife and two daughters. The family regularly shares photos from their vacation, the last one in Cyprus... His wife is an influencer! Moving on to Matt, I find out he resides in Dyke Heights, the very suburban area he grew up in, he is a physics professor. As for Abigail, my search proves futile. She doesn't exist on social media, no online sign whatsoever. The girl *vanished*. My battery is running low. I plug in the phone charger and get up.

I sit at the kitchen table after I get myself a glass of water. My dehydrated mind revisits every line I read, every photo I saw tonight. Perhaps this crime is not supposed to be solved; as a matter of fact, it's hardly understood. No physical evidence, no apparent motive. Who knows, maybe it was an unknown intruder who did this gruesome crime. Sometimes the simplest solution is the best.

CHAPTER 3

Sunday

It's official. The President just declared we are on strict lockdown; citizens should acquire a special permit to leave houses apart from the so-called "key workers." The new measures, she clarified, are taking effect tomorrow morning. It's already ten days since applying my voluntary lockdown, so I guess not much is going to change for me. I'm finishing with the last email as I drink my third cup of tea for today. Time's now 6.17 pm. I can finally relax.

The previous two days had been a nightmare as my thoughts were uncontrollable, and stress took over my existence. Maybe it's the home isolation to blame or specific waves of electromagnetic fields, who knows. At least now, my mood has started to undeniably improve, and I feel much more functional.

"Babe, a courier is here, looking for Ariadne Foster," Mark interrupts my wandering mind.

My books arrived just in time. I even ordered an adult drawing book, hoping it would alleviate my anxiety. But what I'm more excited about is a psychological thriller, the novel by my favorite German author. I unpack the box, everything is there, including an illustrated discount coupon for the next order.

Mark seems concerned. His team faces technical hitches with the application launch, and sluggish internet isn't much of help. He sits in his chair, staring at his desktop screen and holds his chin up.

"I need to go for a walk to clear my mind," he says as he looks for his sneakers.

The door closes, and I'm left alone with my thoughts.

✳ ✳ ✳

Gazing at the cupboards in the kitchen, I wonder what to cook. We had sweet potato soup for lunch, perhaps spaghetti tonight? My phone vibrates as incoming messages are delivered. Alex sends a few from her latest collage artwork; the annual contest is approaching, and competition is rising probably due to home isolation. Meanwhile, in the somewhat euphemistically named group chat "CORGIES," my cousins are unstoppable, a torrent of hysterical NSFW videos flowing on my screen. The water is boiling already, I toss the spaghetti and set the timer. I get back to the living room.

As I place the novels in the bookcase, the coupon falls on the floor; I pick it up and observe it for a few seconds. The colorful logo goes, *"Can you crack the code? Claim 25% off your next 'Scope' purchase!!"* and displays the store's URL link. I visit the page on my phone to find a 25-piece puzzle waiting to be assorted. Why not... *Three. Two more*. It's done! I receive an email with an activated discount.

✽ ✽ ✽

Marks returns from his brief walk, noticeably calmer; he almost looks content.

"Babe guess who just Facebook suggested me to connect with!" he gasps as he locks the door.

"Enlighten me."

"Steve Hunn!"

✽ ✽ ✽

I lie in bed watching a docuseries about a man who stands trial accused of murdering his wife. In this episode, his children are interviewed and support the innocence of their father, sharing anecdotes and describing the serene family life they led. Mark walks into the room to join me.

"What's the case?"

"The trial of Howard Berenson. Remember? It's the second episode. Do you mind?"

"No, it's fine Ariadne, I'll keep up with the plot."

After a quick search online, Mark utters: "At least he got a trial."

The episode wraps up with Howard's children sharing a glimpse of their lives, now highlighting how public scrutiny affected their mental health and overall well-being throughout the years.

"I need to see Jason Oldman's story in a documentary," Mark states sardonically.

"Pity, he avoids publicity."

"I wonder what happened to the children..."

"I looked them up the other night!"

"And?" Mark asks impatiently.

"Oh well, the sons carried on with their lives apparently, only the daughter... Guess what," I pause for a second.

"She's dead?"

"Nope. She's vanished, at least her digital print. Apart from basic graduation public information, not a single online entry is available corresponding to her name."

"Maybe she's changed it."

"It's possible. Though Abigail would still follow her brothers on social media, I believe."

"You searched that too?"

"Baby, please, you know me. Of course, I did but found nothing. No one named Abigail is connected to Matt and George. Or Cynthia. The only thing I can't be sure about Cynthia, she's an internet public figure."

"Who's Cynthia again?"

"George's wife. They live happily married in

Amman with their daughters. Oh, wait, in Zarqa."

"You did your research, Ariadne."

"I think I deserve a treat for this quality of information," I add rascally.

"Treat as in night-time peanut butter-chocolate pancakes?"

My face produces a blissful smile.

A Frothy Algorithm

It's been a rough morning. Everyone is inexplicably on edge today. Neurotic emails and grumpy phone calls have been overwhelming me since 8.30 am. We are in the living room, each one absorbed in a different screen. My head feels heavy, and my sight's resolution begins to compromise. All those tables and excel sheets in front of me, but eventually, it's all autonomous digits, no further connected numbers. My attempts to concentrate prove hopeless. It's time to close my laptop and engage with a non-tech activity.

It's been two months since I started this puzzle on the dining table; it took me two days to figure the frame, and then suddenly, I lost interest. Perhaps I was supposed to, so I have an extra pastime during the pandemic, I think, while inspecting the pieces and sorting them by color. The old-fashioned illustration depicts a lively group of neighbors in a British suburb waiting to get on a red bus. An image otherwise ordinary, yet the ambiance is so anticipated. I reflect on how the sense of time has altered those past weeks. Certain days pass in a flash, whereas some minutes last for hours.

Mark is in the kitchen doing the dishes; I hear the boiler sound. A cup of tea would be much appreciated now. Since the quarantine routine began, I found myself enjoying less coffee and more tea as a pick-me-up, especially English breakfast infusion. Before I finish my thought, Mark comes back with the much-desired hot drink.

"These conspiracy theories are going crazy! Did you see the article on 'The Spectator,' Ariadne?"

"You bet I have."

Of course, it's tempting to get attached to such a mindset in times like this. Books, TV shows, not to mention perfectly-timed documentary premieres, have set the tone for the upcoming events. The ruling lords of the universe implementing little Easter eggs in our reality now and then to keep us alert, right?

"There's a term for this, I think," Mark mutters.

"Predictive programming. It's interesting though, what originally started as a legitimate hypothesis was later used by conspiracy theorists to support their far-fetched concepts. Maybe a little of this tangle holds some truth. I don't know."
Mark agreeably shakes his head. "And then it's the simulation hypothesis," I continue.

"Your favorite one."

"It explains a lot, don't you think?"

✻ ✻ ✻

I laze lethargically on the couch. On TV, a random movie from the 80s is streaming, and Mark is immersed in his phone next to me.

"She's a nun!" he cries all of a sudden.

"No, she's a dentist! Do you pay any attention at all?"

"What are you talking about? I mean, Abigail! She's become a nun. I just found out on Twitter. A former schoolmate spread the word."

"You think it's legit?"

"Looks so. It explains her social absence."

"It's possible."

"Don't underplay the significance of that. Just because you missed the opportunity to claim such a discovery."

"Ok, I'll credit you this tad of victory. As long as you cook lunch."

✻ ✻ ✻

I enter the kitchen and come across a mess. Tomato sauce spilled all over the floor and appliances, Mark is over the pan nervously stirring whatever is inside. I immediately reverse my action and return to the living room. I sit on his chair in front of the desktop. *Change of scenery*. I wonder what's happening on YouTube these days. As soon as I log in, I find out gurus of all fields have posted numerous videos reflecting on the global tragedy, sharing their updated routines and quarantine-inspired culinary tips. What stands out is a frothy coffee recipe. *Dalgona coffee*. Everyone's making it. A few minutes later, I am utterly driven by the algorithm to more foamy creations.

"Baby, the pasta is ready," a voice interrupts my lathered roaming.

I hope the mess is taken care of as I walk into the kitchen.

❋ ❋ ❋

The sauce proves to be scrumptious and pairs well with Prosecco. Regularly I wouldn't drink alcohol during lunch, but today my spirit needs a lift from the damaging effect of external pressure and redundant grumbles. And this glass of wine does the trick.

"Love, it's delicious. If the crypto business doesn't work out, you have, beyond doubt, a considerable gastronomic potential!"

"What a reassuring remark," he sighs, to continue, "and you Ariadne Foster might as well pursue an alternative career as a private investigator in case you get furloughed."

"I have the appropriate background," I laugh defensively.

"Now, you believe the case can be solved after twenty years?"

"As time goes by, it becomes harder to find additional evidence or get new testimonies. But it's worth searching and evaluating clues from a different perspective, even reassess the original investigation itself in a retrospective manner."

"The sweet taste of criticism."

"As I ruminate on the case, the more certain I am; the killer had an accomplice."

"Elaborate, please."

"See, according to the forensic reports, the women likely lied on the floor while being stabbed; if you consider the fact that no defensive wounds were found, it means someone was holding the victims while they were being attacked. Otherwise, the circumstances must have been enormously favorable to the predator."

"I hope Jason Oldman confesses in his death-bed. His children deserve the truth. We deserve the truth," Mark exhales as he opens the fridge looking for, presumably, dessert.

CHAPTER 4

Meal Decoding

"Do you need anything from the '*Scope*'?" I ask Mark as I'm about to submit my order.

"Hmm, a flash drive for sure. How much for 256 Giga?"

"No worries babe, I have a coupon 25% off," I add proudly.

"How come?"

"I solved a puzzle the other day."

"Fantastic."

A final click, and I'm done! Three more books to arrive next week, including a flash drive and an azure water bottle. I look for my phone; it's under the couch next to a dead battery smartwatch. *Great.*

I move to the kitchen, contemplating what kind of hot drink to consume next. Chamomile? Too calmative. Earl grey tea? Too strong. I search the back of the cupboard; that's it, cocoa! As the water boils, my memory goes back to Paris. The hotel we stayed at had a vending machine serving coffee and hot chocolate, only the chocolate option never worked. Every morning I pushed the button for chocolate anticipating it'd been fixed, every time I got disappointed. What's the saying? Paranoia is doing the same thing over and over again, expecting different results or something.

I once more find myself semi-lying on the couch with my laptop in front of me.

"So, what puzzle you solved?"

"A promotional code from 'Scope,'" I grin.

He processes my answer for a few seconds and then comes to join the idleness. At this point, we are both lying on our backs, gazing at the light beige ceiling. I close my eyes, and gleaming mandalas begin to form behind my retina.

"Didn't the FBI once share a coded message with the public to help in decryption?" Mark interrupts my mental drawing.

"I think so. Like nine, ten years ago?"

"Is it still online? Let me see," he adds while typing.

The experimental launch of 'QuantiCoin' this morning was slightly disappointing. Mark prefers to crack codes instead of writing one at the moment. I get it.

"Nope, I can't find anything," he sighs.

"The headquarters should consider uploading a case or two for the poor home-quarantined detectives like us."

"Sherlock or Watson? Who you choose to be?" he asks mischievously.

"Watson. That makes you Sherlock."

* * *

The doorbell rings.

"Our groceries are here," I shout from the shower.

"I got it, babe!"

Luckily, the sweet potatoes came precisely on time. I get out of the bathroom and quickly change into my red plait pajama pants and a grey T-shirt. I find Mark in the kitchen arranging the edible arrivals.

"Potatoes with garlic and cheese for dinner?" he suggests eagerly.

"And Brussel sprouts."

We pop everything on a tray, and our precious meal enters the oven. Mark sets the clock and returns to his computer to continue his online pursuit.

As I brush my wet hair, I stumble on a tenacious tangle. *This cannot be happening.* Meantime, my phone is buzzing; The CORGIES are back. Another uproarious video! CORGIES were officially created two years ago after a venturesome summer, Emma, John, and I spent in our hometown, Peninsula Port. In the past few days, the homonymous group chat has been proved to be of excellent mental value. Home isolation itself proves not such a challenge after all; as a matter of fact, I often find myself savoring it. It's the plethora of external stress that kills my spirit. Financial uncertainty, endless calls, emails at unsuitable hours, and the adverse feeling that work toxicity has invaded my home asylum. Suddenly, the phone tinkles again, email from work this time. *Brilliant.*

I just finished the diagrams, and now I swiftly compose a workmanlike email. I press 'send' and hope for the best; no one disturbs me for at least 12 hours. That was some nerve! But no, I won't let it spoil my evening. Wait, what's that smell? Oh my! *Dinner!*

Mark is already in the kitchen, trying to save the day. The vegetables on the bottom clearly have no hope. Totally burnt. Mark looks devastated as he carefully examines the cooking tray.

"How did this happen?" he sulkily murmurs.
"I didn't catch the timer at all," I reply in an apologetic tone. Did I hear it? I can't recall. "What about you, babe? Did you hear anything?" He doesn't respond. At least, the top layer seems to bear a decent potential for making it onto our plates.

❊ ❊ ❊

Luckily the disaster wasn't extensive. With the addition of some freshly chopped salad and a few crackers, our meal is successfully served.

"What are we watching tonight? Movie or series?"

"I don't mind, Mark. Anything."

"Do you think it's too much garlic?"

"No, it's fine. Tasty. No one would tell it almost burnt," I comment as I take another bite. But before I swallow, it hits me. *Burnt.* I get up.

"Ariadne, what's wrong?"

"Burnt, Mark. That's what's wrong."

"I don't understand."

"How long were the potatoes in the oven? Forty? Forty-five minutes?"

"Make it fifty."

"The real question is not who cooks a stew at six in the morning but who burns one at 12.30 pm!" Mark is staring at me, baffled.

"You lost me."

"Stews require hours to cook. If it was put in the oven at 6.30, even 6 am, it wouldn't be ready until 12- or even later. How long does it take to bake a stew? Google it!"

"Ok, I'm searching now, take a breath," he utters while typing. "Uhm, meantime is four hours but can reach up to eight, if the stew is in a slow cooker." I quickly go to the bedroom and open my laptop. Where's that blog? Uh right. Scrolling down, evidence, right!

"Mark! It's a slow cooker!" I scream both scared and delighted.

❋ ❋ ❋

I wriggle nervously in the living room as I try to figure out what my fresh discovery actually means.

"Ariadne, take a breath, and let's resume."

"Ok, right," I sigh and take a seat on the couch. "What we now know for a fact is that the cooking time is at least six hours, maybe eight. This means if Stephanie or Eleanor put it in the cooker at 6.30, it would be ready around 12, if not later."

"And under no circumstances, burnt down by 12.30."

"Right."

"So, this suggests the cookery began much earlier, maybe 4 am?"

"That's one explanation," I mutter as I juggle the possibilities.

"Therefore, the husband lied about the time they woke up."

"Or," I ecstatically add, "he is even more diabolical than that. Stephanie would unquestionably set the right temperature and time, but what if she wasn't the one who switched it on?"

"The killer?!"

"Imagine that, what if the murders took place around six. Before Jason leaves the house, he puts the food in the cooker- if it wasn't already in-and turns the device on. He intends on everyone believing that something interrupted the peaceful cookery."

"But he messes with the settings. This explains the black smoke at 12.30."

"Exactly. Jason doesn't know how long a stew actually takes to make since he's never cooked."

CHAPTER 5

Yellow Notice

I scroll down on Instagram, envying the perfect chromatically-aligned book collections that appear in my newsfeed. It's 11.35 am, the phone lacks any notifications, and an espresso *americano* lays right in front of me on the coffee table. Bliss.

Last night's startling revelations kept us up late, trying to understand how this finding could have an impact on the case today. Such a little detail, completely overlooked for eighteen years, could it had been regarded as circumstantial evidence? Most likely, we'll never know. But what we know for sure is that Jason Oldman lied. Maybe this won't do justice to the victims, but at least our snooping spirits are satisfied for the time being.

Mark is at his desk enjoying a cup of coffee, too, while researching, what I presume to be, marketing articles. He seems kind of rejuvenated today.

"Ariadne, remember those escape-themed board games?"

"Oh, yes! Are we getting one?"

"Check the link I sent you."

To my surprise, he has already ordered not one but two "EXIT" games. The first one is appropriately themed and requires the players to prevent the spreading of a lethal virus out of a classified lab. In the second, the player, who supposedly works for Interpol, hunts a notorious jewelry thief. I've always felt great gratitude towards game creators; for designing alternative universes, we can anytime immerse into and entertain ourselves escaping, in essence, reality. But for now, I have to go back to the charts and numbers.

✣ ✣ ✣

The soup is almost ready. Carrots and sweet potatoes have proved exceptional mood boosters over time, so they'll do the trick once again. Mark just chopped the salad, and the bread is heating in the oven. Another quiet afternoon is unfolding in our household.

"Are we watching anything?"

"Anything but warfare, babe," I quickly respond.

"So be it then."

An infamous drug lord is marching on-screen, the ideal lunch company. The documentary narrates the works and days of Dominique Shehu, before his eventful arrest in 2004. At this point, my eyes feel hefty, and I want to curl up in bed. But I'd better stay awake if I care to salvage my circadian rhythm. Subsequently, I need coffee. *Perhaps coffee needs me as well*, I think, as I toss seven ice cubes in a glass.

"Ariadne, what are you muttering?"

"Uh, no. I was thinking of something. Did you hear me talk? I don't know, I'm so drowsy."

"Babe, look at this. Dominique is currently the most wanted person, and his third wife is number two!"

"The 'Bonnie and Clyde' of opium."

"Including all accomplices."

"Where's that again?"

He points to the screen and adds: "On Interpol.com."

❊ ❊ ❊

It's been at least twenty minutes of aimless browsing, searching criminals per crime, sex, or country. Records go even sixty years back. Caffeine begins to take effect, finally. My brain rouses as, on the top right of the page, I see a yellow square.

"What's that?" I wonder as I click on it, and Mark approaches the monitor curiously. *Yellow Notice: Missing Persons.*

The page format is similar to the previous one, only mugshots are replaced with selfies and vacation pictures. And most notably, these images portray mainly children. Hundreds of thousands of children and teenagers around the globe have their forlornly online profiles filled with details concerning their outfits and whereabouts the day they went missing. *That day.* What was the last thing they saw, what crossed their minds those final seconds before their disappearance, or worse, their deaths?

I experiment with the search filters, and when I reach the location field, my fingertips type "Peninsula Port." I get only one result, as I may have expected. Nathan Ericson. All of a sudden, I get the chills as memories leap out from a hiding place of my consciousness.

About Nathan

Nathan was six years old when he mysteriously vanished from the front yard. The noon of July 13th, 1996, his mother Vicki had just picked him up from the daycare and was inside the house with husband Alan and little Liam. Nathan was playing outside alone, and after his mother called him repeatedly to join them for lunch, she decided to fetch him herself. What she found was a couple of toy trucks and his left shoe.

Alan wasn't Nathan's biological father. I don't have to consult the internet for this information because I knew them, we lived in the same neighborhood. Vicki, a Finnish citizen, had relocated with Nathan to Peninsula Port two years ago. She met Alan, and after a couple of months, she got pregnant. The couple moved into the neighborhood soon after she gave birth to Liam. Both Vicki and Alan worked in a catering company.

My sister had befriended Nathan, and I would often join them to supervise their play, as the big sister. Only that summer, my family and I were in our grandparent's summer house in Red Isle. I distinctly remember that blistering sultry morning, the phone ringing and a couple of minutes later, my mom turning pale. From what we heard, Vicki started looking immediately for Nathan in the neighborhood, went to a nearby abandoned house the kids used to play at all the time. He was nowhere. After approximately an hour, she finally called the police. But Nathan was for good gone.

The case attracted local interest but not the media's attention. Usually, mainstream reporters are mostly fascinated by toddlers, especially young girls' disappearances. Undeniably, a tabloid frenzy wouldn't have put much in the case and was auspiciously avoided. Interest gradually faded for young Nathan, and to this day, over twenty years later, no one knows what truly happened to him.

❊ ❊ ❊

Engrossed in my screen dragging old articles up, I hear Mark scolding me.

"Ariadne, that's enough sleuthing for today. It's

been three hours."

"Huh?"

"End of the investigation. Game over. We are watching a movie tonight. Pick one."

"Yes, I'm done. Adding a few more bookmarks, and I call it a day."

I finish up, swiftly close my laptop, and take my favorite seat on the couch.

"Ready? So, what are we streaming?"

"The Man Who Knew Too Much," I reply determinedly.

❀ ❀ ❀

The movie is over. Mark looks at me and states in a reasonably sarcastic tone:

"Ok, consider your agenda passed. We'll delve into every detail tomorrow."

CHAPTER 6

Wednesday Morning

Wait, fever? *Again?* My body aches, I get the chills and my head burns. I abandon a freshly brewed coffee and retire to bed. The time is now 9.30 am. Mark enters the bedroom and looks at me, skeptically.

"That job, Ariadne. That triggers your illness."

"I feel so stiff. Get me some acetaminophen babe."

I swallow the pills and text the zoom group before closing my eyes again.

I twirl under the duvet seeking my phone. 11.40 am, no messages. *Thank God.* The pain is gone, so is the cephalalgia. I gaze at the balcony door and decide to get up. I'm home alone. Once again, I take my chances with coffee, I need the caffeine stimulus to carry on this doomed day. At least I have no work commitments for today.

I have moved my weary self to the living room, searching for a suitable online stream, in vain. Myriad of options, but apparently, I'm not in the mood for that. I hear keys in the lock, and Mark, with a mask on his face, enters the hall carrying two bags from the bakery.

"I went to the pharmacy. I also got a few baguettes and pretzels. How are you doing?"

"Better. You fancy any coffee?"

"Nah, I'm good."

I join as he prepares an appetizing parmesan snack.

"Do you have a meeting today?"

"I had one. Eric made a few adjustments to the code; we are running another test tomorrow. I presume you took the day off, Ariadne."

"You assume right," I reply while squeezing an orange.

"That suggests our investigation is on?"

My eyes immediately twinkle, and a shiver runs through my body. Only this time, it's not a fever.

❅ ❅ ❅

We are in the living room now, over the coffee table, with a fully charged laptop and a notepad. On TV, news updates play in the background. Mark is going through the bookmarks I pinned the night before.

"Nine articles? That's all?" he asks, irritated. I shrug and take the last sip of my coffee.

"I need a cup of tea. Want some?"

"Ariadne, you are an addict."

"I'm well aware of that."

The boiler is heating, a dilemma regarding herbal infusions occupies my mind, as I envision Wilma and Nathan playing in our backyard on a sunshiny afternoon. An actual moment from the past or a fictitious memory? I pop an earl grey teabag in the mug and return to the coffee table.

"We have scarce data to work with, Ariadne," Mark points out as he scribbles on the notepad.

"Don't give up so easily, Sherlock."

"First of all, I can't figure time. Nathan disappeared at noon, but no time frame is disclosed."

"Uhm, I haven't read the articles yet, give me a moment."

"There's not much to see, merely repetitive, vague information. I've found a few videos on YouTube, Vicki re-enacting the events of July the 13th with the assistance of friends and Alan. And an interview she gave to the local TV-station."

❊ ❊ ❊

I look at the screen, concerned. The reports more or less rechew the same knowledge, and except for three of them, the rest add nothing further to the case.

"Ok, let's examine them one by one; we'll write down all available information and see what we really get," I say as I type, still bearing a trace of hope.

"Alright, first is the theory that Nathan's biological father kidnapped him. Vicki expressed concerns to the police, though after contacting him in Finland, he claimed full ignorance and sent his sympathies to Vicki."

"Then it's the possibility an accident happened, maybe Nathan went to the streets, a careless driver ran over him and fearing justice, he or she removed the body."

"Last but not least, the worst scenario of all; the parents," he sighs.

My phone rings and interrupts the investigative brainstorming.

A New Suspect

The call led to another call, then an urgent press release from the government aired live on TV, and here we are now at 3.55pm, hungry and indolent. We finally agree on ordering burgers. Our inspective activity has clearly declined, but suddenly the phone buzzes again, a message from Emma.

"It looks like we have another suspect, Mark. Nelson Carlton."

Nelson Carlton, a lawyer and prominent member of the Peninsula Port society, was considered a person of interest during the early investigation days since rumor had it, he had a child molestation past. However, the allegations were never proved, and he was never formally accused of such violation. His name was certainly not publicly connected to Nathan's disappearance out of discretion and fear of defamation. But Emma remembered her parents' discussions back then and provided me with this valuable information.

✳ ✳ ✳

"So, Ariadne, what's the deal with Nelson?"

"He was nearby the house that day, in his car. Emma says it was Mrs. Kennel who saw him."

"Mrs. Kennel?"

"Louise Kennel. The local pharmacist, remember we saw her earlier in the videos. She saw Nelson twice in the sideway with the engine turned off!"

"Was he questioned by the police?"

"We'll have more information in a while."

"Ok, so we have Nathan's dad, Alan, and Nelson. I'd eliminate the dad since we don't even know his first name, and the fact he was physically in Finland at the time is a considerable burden."

"Agreed," I answer as I message Emma.

"Alan. Where's the dude now?"

We find Vicki's social media, and the research becomes more suspenseful and vigorous. She now lives in Helsinki with two dogs, and apparently owns a café in the city. Liam is in the Netherlands and has a girlfriend, Selma. He mainly works as a security guard in boxing tournaments. Only, no clue for Alan Riggs. He disappeared as well. The somewhat fruitless online espionage disturbs the door-bell.

* * *

The time is now 6 pm. Sitting on the couch, gazing the news, dissatisfied with our recent discoveries, or else the lack of any, we are waiting for the miraculous clue, *a Deux ex machina*.

"Do you think he's alive, Aria?"

"Alan?"

"No, Nathan."

"Most likely, Nathan is dead. And most certainly we are on a wild goose chase. Whoever did it won't be uncovered by a couple of amateur sleuths, over twenty years later, who sit on a sofa, in front of a TV, petting their bellies!"

My phone vibrates as Emma sends some more information.

"Oh my god, Mark. Listen to this, Nelson was questioned by the police, allegedly had some sort of alibi, and the cherry on top, he was besties with the police chief. No, I take that back! The best part is that he's dead!"

* * *

A headache has begun to torture me as if the afternoon failure wasn't enough. Should I go back to my excel sheets? As I scroll pointlessly, I consider how detective life can be awfully disappointing and frustrating. But an ad banner on Instagram thinks otherwise. A simple "click" will soon transfuse an entirely new perspective to the case.

Guilts

I sit on my vanity desk, looking at the screen astounded. *Is it possible?* My brain burns, though I can't deny the thrill. I sit up, grab my laptop, and join Mark in the living room.

"Babe, I found out something. As a matter of fact, I might have found out *everything*."
He joins me on the couch, enthralled by the statement.

"See, I came across this book ad earlier," I explain while showing Mark the webpage.

"What's that? 'Aching Souls'?"

"By?"

"Louise Martha Kennel."

"It's about child abuse. Louise is a strong advocate, she has written another two books, and has participated in numerous podcasts on the matter."

"So?"

"I listened to a few extracts and guess what. She's obsessed with Nathan. She did it, Mark. Louise killed Nathan; the least, she's sinisterly involved."

"Because she wrote a book on child abuse?"

"She has written three books, talks about him at every opportunity, and there is this blog post," I add finger-pointing the screen.

"She accused Vicki of neglecting Nathan? But they were friends! Louise was by her side all the time, helped her with the reporters and police, oh…", Mark sighs.

"Right *at all times.* She wasn't interested in Vicki's well-being. She wanted an insight into the investigation."

"Sketchy behavior."

"Exactly. And this confirmed my theory ten minutes ago," I say as I hand Mark my phone to see Emma's last text.

"Unbelievable. Louise and Nelson had inheritance disputes? So, she had a motive to frame him!"

"Right! Distant hostile cousins. Louise said she saw him as she passed by. *Twice.* If this statement is true, what reason she had to be there in the first place?"

About Louise Kennel

Louise, the well-loved pharmacist, and devout Christian, involved in a child's disappearance? Suddenly, my childhood becomes violated as I recollect the birthday parties spent at her home by the beach. Her sons went to the same school as my sister and I, subsequently, we were invited often to such celebrations, even our parents paid her a visit from time to time. Mrs. Kennel had widowed at a young age, just a few days after she gave birth to her youngest son.

In the early nineties, she inherited a significant segment of coastal land and built a house. *That house.*

"Daydreaming, Ariadne?"

"I was thinking of Louise. She must have retired by now. Last summer, I passed by her house, a mansion to be precise, it was renovated. I think she turned it into an inn."

"Where's that exactly?" Mark asks as he opens Google maps.

"Baby, you are brilliant! There, the last house on the coast, on the left."

"I see a pool, she's clearly well-off, and wait who has a church in their back garden?"

"Louise, apparently."

CHAPTER 7

Doubts

I reluctantly open my eyes. An unbearable bright light emerges from the shutters. Laughs, loud voices, and canary tweets are heard through the balcony. I get up and open the door. My neighbors are lavishly savoring the vitamin D production, in colorful outfits, while flinging themselves in video calls. I suppose it must be noon already. I slept around six in the morning; thus, best-case scenario, time is now somewhere between 12.30 to 1.15 pm. I go back inside to check my phone; the time is precisely 1.03 pm.

I can use double the espresso dose today. In the past few days, my biological clock has deteriorated for good, almost as if I put myself in a voluntary and unnecessary jet lag. I feel lightheaded and cold. I can't even remember what kept us up so late. I pop a couple more ice cubes in the glass, grab the thermometer, and return to the balcony with my cherished beverage. As I sit and enjoy my drink, I reflect on how rare this moment feels, though it's a customary Sunday activity. Drinking coffee on the terrace and measuring your temperature, what's so extraordinary about it? I look around the apartments and observe the tenants cautiously. What are their evil secrets, if any? What skeletons do they keep in their closets?

"Ariadne?"

"You woke up, babe?"

"My throat hurts. How are you? Still feverish?"

"It's probably nothing, our sleeping schedule is awful. I feel terrible, as well. But my temperature is normal. Here sit, I'll get you some coffee and vitamin C."

A pile of dirty dishes in the sink asks for my attention, funny I didn't notice earlier. But I opt to ignore it for now. The sound of the effervescent tablet dissolving in a glass of water tickles my head pleasantly as the grinding sound of the coffee machine stops. I return to the balcony; Mark has closed his eyes indulging in the sunlight.

"It's an exquisite day, isn't it, Aria?"

"It is," I sigh as I sit on the chair on his left, "nature is thriving again. After all, it's spring."

"I saw the weirdest dream last night- or earlier today, to be exact. It was Jason Oldman and Louise Kennel on a cruise ship dancing," Mark says as he takes his first espresso sip.

"Wow! That's wild!" I laugh, to continue, "I've been thinking, after all the research we did, their devious manners were exposed, is it enough, though?"

"It's not evidence, under no circumstances, but

still indicative of their actions."

"Besides, it's our reflections on the crimes. How are we sure our conclusions didn't emerge under the distorted lens of home isolation and a desperate need for excitement?"

"No, Watson!" he protests, "You lost faith in us. Why rationalize and cancel our hard-earned deductions? Don't underestimate our brains' capacity."

"It's a gift, I guess. Anyway, these discoveries couldn't add much to the cases' closure."

"At least, we know the truth, Ariadne. I tell you those past weeks were the best thing we could ever ask for, considering the conditions."

A Farce

"Yes, mom. I'll do it. No worries, bye," I sigh as I end the call.
Perfect. Taxes are the last thing I need to amuse my mind. I join Mark on the couch while he's absorbed, watching the news. His expression has noticeably changed the last twenty minutes.

"Why so serious, babe?"

"I don't know, Aria, the reality is starting to get me."

"Just switch it off. Let's see a movie, series, whatever. Something uplifting, with no animal abuse. And we make salty pancakes."

"Ok, it's a deal!"

* * *

It seems like our spirits are irreversibly gloomy. We are lying on the couch, distracted from the plot, lost in our thoughts. We have succumbed ourselves to what seems to be a movie marathon, without satisfactory results. I get up and go to the bookcase, maybe a novel could put an end to my boredom and distress. My mind should stay busy at all times, that's a decision I took early on, the first days of quarantine provided that I wanted to preserve my sanity.

"What about some hot cocoa?" I suggest.

"Sure. I want mine with milk."

"Absolutely, sir."

As the water boils, I look for my favorite travel mug, nowhere to be found, I have to settle for the runner-up. Maybe some cookies too? Right! I put everything on a tray and rush to the living room, hoping this warm potion will boost our mood.

"Did I miss anything?"

"His wife died."

"Splendid. I'll focus on my book now. No more TV for me today."

Page 133, the inspector questions a key witness; I remember that paragraph. Gradually, I immerse myself in the story as I join the world-famous detective Ignatius Figgs in a thrillingly cerebral adventure.

✳ ✳ ✳

Suddenly the phone buzzes, disrupting an unforeseen fictional confession. I indifferently unlock it to see a notification from John, another prank video, maybe? But as soon as I open the freshly delivered message, I freeze.

Sometimes, unexpected things happen. An unannounced event that changes the story's route, or even creates the story in the first place. *A serendipitous incident, a fortunate accident.* A godsent hand of help, perhaps? Or a coincidence. Are coincidences genuinely random? Is there such thing as coincidence after all, or is it part of a meticulously executed existential farce? No matter how we may interpret it, such a startling event just occurred.

"Mark, open the TV, channel Six."

"What happened?"

"Channel Six," I urge him.

"...authorities have cordoned off the area, as the investigation continues for the human bones found in the chapel. According to initial reports, the skeleton apparently belongs to a preschooler, presumably a boy. Forensic pathologist Dr. Stewart is expected to give a briefing tomorrow morning at 9 am. With regard to the dead bodies, police have initiated a formal inquiry to ascertain the circumstances of the events..."

We look at each other flabbergasted and baffled.

CHAPTER 8

The Aftermath

I struggle to wake up. I look at the clock, it's 9.40 am. *Great.* The only positive, today's meeting was canceled so I can fully commit to any updates concerning the recent revelations.

Last night we witnessed a tragic yet exhilarating turn of events. As we learned, Louise Kennel had become sick three days ago and was admitted to the hospital where she was diagnosed with the coronavirus infection. On Saturday, she was transferred to ICU due to complications. What we also came to know is she operated a small nursing home where her house used to be; the coastal mansion had turned into an elder care facility.

The local authorities obliged to perform the essential disinfection protocol; only when the cleaning employees got to the accommodations, they came across a heartbreaking encounter. Three tenants were found dead, whereas another two were critically ill. Personnel was nowhere to be seen, presumably had left the elderly to their fate. When the employees entered the chapel, they detected a hole in the floor, which was, in fact, an improvised vault. Inside the vault, human bones were found. I haven't read the news yet, but undoubtedly, Dr. Stewart will have already confirmed the bones belong to a little boy.

I finally get up. My muscles hurt, especially the legs. Mark is already up; I hear him talking nervously on the phone. I'd better have a coffee immediately and check my temperature. In the kitchen, the dishes from the day before yesterday still seek my attention. *Maybe later.*

I look at the thermometer. *Damn*, 37.4 °C. Is it self-suggestion, or am I really sweating? I swallow a pill with hot coffee and go to the living room. I open my laptop to confirm the findings of the forensic pathologist and read a couple more enlightening articles on the subject.

"Do you think they'll connect the dots?" Mark joins me as soon as he finishes with his call.

"They already did, Vicki and Liam sent DNA samples."

"But why? What motive did Louise have to kill the boy?"

"I doubt whether we ever find out the truth; most likely, she'll be dead by the end of the week."

Tick Tock

Time's up. The lentil soup must be ready as I hear the

chronometer going off. Mark, in an attempt to ease his stress, has flung himself into culinary creations. The QuantiCoin app is live since 12 pm, and the whole team is on edge.

"Are you hungry, Ariadne?"

"No, babe, not yet."

"Neither am I."

"Is everything going smoothly with the application?"

"So far, so good," he responds as he sits in his chair and switches the desktop on.

"I've been thinking Mark, throughout our investigation, we held a false preconception."

"What's that?"

"Time. For the past weeks, we thought it was against us when, in reality, it was the most valuable piece of proof."

"But can time become a clue?"

"Not only was it a clue, but generated a series of further evidence if you think of it."

He gazes at his screen pensively, and adds: "If this wasn't for the pandemic, Nathan's tragic end wouldn't have unveiled."

✻ ✻ ✻

"Ariadne, what have you done to the algorithm?"

"What's wrong?"

"I get some weird suggestions on YouTube, everyone's mixing and beating sugar with instant coffee. What new fetish is this?"

"Ah, the *dalgona* coffee. It's a huge global trend. Maybe we should try it."

"You try it."

"Ok, just let me see the ingredient analogy," I add as I get up and move toward his desk.

In the perfectly-lit video, a pair of hands with numerous rose gold rings, and bracelets use a mixer to create the frothy recipe. Three teaspoons of instant coffee together with an equal amount of white sugar, mixed for at least two minutes. And then four ice cubes and 120ml of almond milk. First goes the milk with the ice followed by the coffee. My gaze moves from the crafting hands to the video description, *Cynthia's Wardrobe- Dalgona The Best Recipe,* and then back to the close-up shot and, more specifically, to the left wrist, which is adorned by a memorable vintage Omega watch.

A MESSAGE TO READERS

Dear Reader,

Thanks for picking this novelette. If you enjoyed the story, I'd genuinely appreciate it if you could take the time and leave a review on Amazon or Goodreads. If you have hints and suggestions for Ariadne, feel free to send them to ariadnefosterinvestigates-@gmail.com. Also, don't forget to wash your hands.

Stay safe!

Catherine

ABOUT THE AUTHOR

Catherine is a true-crime enthusiast and enjoys suspenseful fiction, though, in real life, she'd rather avoid any stress-inducing situation. However, this is not always the case. When she's not following clues or drinking coffee, she fancies going for long walks. She also loves danish rolls.

"What's on True Crime Tonight?" is her first literary attempt.

Visit www.randomlime.com for more!

BOOKS IN THIS SERIES

Mystery and Suspense Files

What's On True Crime Tonight? A Mystery Story

Next Door Murder: The Apartment 8C

Blue Pineapple: A Classified Mystery

Printed in Great Britain
by Amazon